trust me

By Eleanor Robins

SADDLEBACK
EDUCATIONAL PUBLISHING

SADDLEBACK
EDUCATIONAL PUBLISHING
www.sdlback.com

Copyright © 2011 by Saddleback Educational Publishing

ISBN-13: 978-1-61651-599-7
ISBN-10: 1-61651-599-6
eBook: 978-1-61247-245-4

Printed in Guangzhou, China
0411/04-25-11

15 14 13 12 11   1 2 3 4 5

Meet the Characters from

trust me

Emma: a student at Trenton High, Jordyn's best friend, dates Darius

Jordyn: a student at Trenton High, Emma's best friend, on the debate team

Darius: a student at Camden High, on the debate team at Camden, dates Emma

Emma's Mom: drives Emma and Jordyn home

Mrs. Chen: the debate team advisor at Trenton High

chapter 1

It was Monday morning. Emma was on her way to school. She went to Trenton High.

Her mom was driving her to school.

Emma said, "I can hardly wait to get to school. I hope Jordyn is already there."

"Why?" her mom asked.

"I'm in a hurry to talk to Jordyn," Emma said.

Jordyn was her best friend.

Emma and her family had been out of town all weekend. And she had not talked to any of her friends since Friday.

Emma said, "I want to ask Jordyn who won the debate. We got home too late last night for me to call her."

The debate team had a big debate over the weekend. And four teams were in the debate.

Jordyn was on the debate team. So Emma knew she would know which team won.

Emma hoped it was Trenton High.

Her mom stopped the car in front of the school. And Emma quickly got out of the car.

Emma said, "Bye, Mom. Thanks for the ride."

"Have a good day," her mom said.

"You too, Mom," Emma said.

Emma closed the car door. Then she looked for Jordyn. But she didn't see her.

Emma hoped Jordyn was already at school. And she had gone to her first class.

Emma hurried up the walkway to the school. She started to walk to her first class.

Emma had the same first class that Jordyn did. And she also had a class with Jordyn right before lunch.

Emma got to her classroom. And she hurried into the room. She saw Jordyn.

Emma walked over to her desk. And she sat down. She and Jordyn sat next to each other.

Jordyn said, "Did you have a good time this weekend, Emma?"

"I guess. But I wanted to be here. I wanted to call you last night. But I got home too late to call or text," Emma said.

"I thought that was why you didn't call," Jordyn said.

Emma said, "So who won the debate? Did we win?"

But Jordyn didn't look excited. So Emma didn't think Trenton High won.

"We did a great job. I guess I shouldn't brag about my own team like that," Jordyn said. "But we did do a great job. And Mrs. Chen said we did a great job too."

Mrs. Chen was the debate coach.

"But we didn't win. We came in second. And I'm sure you can guess which team won. Camden High. We never can beat them. But I guess you're sort of glad they won," Jordyn said.

Emma knew why Jordyn said that.

"You know I always want our team to win, Jordyn. But our team didn't win. So, yes, I'm glad Camden beat us," said Emma. "And not some other team. Did Darius do a great job?"

Darius was Emma's boyfriend. And he was on the debate team at Camden High.

"Darius always does great. That's one reason why Camden always beats us," Jordyn said.

"But you said we came in second. That's still good news," Emma said.

"I know. Camden gets to go to the state finals. And we get to go too," Jordyn said.

"So maybe we'll win then," Emma said.

Jordyn laughed. But it wasn't a happy laugh.

"No way. We have one little problem," Jordyn said.

"What?" Emma asked.

"The little problem is Camden High. Their team is too good. And there's no way we can beat them," Jordyn said.

"Don't think that way, Jordyn. Or our team will lose for sure," Emma said.

"You know we'll all do the best we

can. But it just won't be good enough. But there's one thing for you to be happy about," Jordyn said.

"What?" Emma asked. But she thought she knew why Jordyn said that.

"Your boyfriend's team will win. So it won't be all bad for you," Jordyn said.

"I like Darius a lot. And I want him to do well. But I go to Trenton High. Not Camden High. And I want our team to win," Emma said.

chapter 2

It was the next day. The end of school bell rang. Emma and Jordyn hurried out of the school.

Emma had a lot of books. Jordyn did too. And Jordyn had a thick folder full of papers on top of her books.

Emma's mom was picking them up after school. So both girls looked for her car.

Emma said, "I see Mom's car."

"I see it too," Jordyn said.

The two girls started to walk quickly to the car.

Jordyn was walking too fast. And the folder slid off of her books. And it started to fall to the ground. The folder opened. And many papers fell on the ground.

Jordyn started to pick up some of the papers. Emma started to help Jordyn. And they both began to put the papers back in the folder.

Jordyn said, "Thanks for helping me pick up all of this, Emma."

"Glad to help. What's this folder? It sure does have a lot of papers in it," Emma said.

Jordyn said, "It's my debate folder. It has my debate notes in it. And some of the research I use to get ready for the debates."

The girls picked up all of the papers. And they put them in the folder.

Then they hurried over to the car. They quickly got in the car. And Emma's mom started to drive away from the school.

They rode for a few minutes. And Emma and Jordyn talked about school.

Then Emma's mom said, "Last night Emma told me the good news, Jordyn. That your debate team will be in the state finals. Good luck next week. I hope Trenton High wins."

"Thanks. But I don't think we'll win," Jordyn said.

"Why not?" Emma's mom asked.

"Because of Emma's boyfriend," Jordyn said.

"Darius? How will he keep you from winning?" Emma's mom asked.

"Because we'll debate Camden High. And Darius is the best one on the team. And he always wins his debates," Jordyn said.

"Emma told me Darius is on the Camden High team. But I didn't know he was that good," Emma's mom said.

"He is. I don't know who will debate him one on one. But I'm glad it won't be me," Jordyn said.

"I'm sure you would do well if you did," Emma's mom said.

"Who do you think will debate Darius?" Emma asked.

"I don't know," Jordyn said.

"Then how do you know it won't be you?" Emma's mom asked.

"Darius is a senior. And I'm only a junior," Jordyn said. "So Mrs. Chen will pick one of the seniors to debate him. And for once I'm glad I'm not a senior."

"Who do you think she should pick?" Emma asked.

"I don't know. Maybe Seth. But no one on our team is really good enough to beat

Darius. And that's why I think Camden High will win the debate," Jordyn said.

Emma said, "But you don't know that for sure, Jordyn. And the team still has over a week to practice before the debate."

Jordyn said, "I know. But I don't think practicing will do that much good against Darius."

Emma's mom said, "How often does the team practice, Jordyn?"

"One afternoon a week most weeks. And twice a week the two weeks before a debate," Jordyn said.

Emma's mom said, "That sounds like a lot of extra work for you. Why do you want to be on the debate team?"

Jordyn laughed. Then she said, "For a very good reason. I like to argue with people."

"That's for sure," Emma said.

Jordyn liked to argue a lot with her. But sometimes Emma liked to argue too. So she and Jordyn didn't get mad at each other.

Jordyn laughed again. Then she said, "And sometimes that gets me into trouble. I don't mean to be rude. I just like to argue. And a debate is a good way to argue with people. And not get into trouble when I do."

Emma's mom said, "Emma likes to argue too. Maybe Emma should be on the debate team too."

Emma laughed. And so did her mom and Jordyn.

chapter 3

It was the next day. Emma was at school. She was in her last class.

The end of school bell rang.

Emma hurried out of her classroom. She quickly walked to her locker. She saw Jordyn. Jordyn was at her locker. Her locker was next to Emma's locker.

Emma said, "I'm glad school is over. I'm in a hurry to get home. I have a lot of homework to do. And I want to get started on it."

"I'm glad I don't have a lot of homework for my classes. I want to work on some things for the debate next week. And I need as much time as I can get for that," Jordyn said.

"Are you still worried about that?" Emma asked. But she was sure Jordyn was.

"Yeah, you know me. I like to argue a lot. And I worry a lot too," Jordyn said.

"Don't worry. And argue only when you debate," Emma said.

Jordyn laughed. "I will try to do that. But don't count on it," Jordyn said.

Emma and Jordyn got some books out of their lockers. Then they closed their lockers. They started to walk down the hall.

Both girls had a lot of books. And Jordyn had her debate folder too.

The girls got to the front door of the

school. And they walked out of the school.

Emma looked for her mom's car. She saw it right away.

Emma said, "I see Mom's car. Hold on to all of your things today, Jordyn. And don't drop your debate folder."

"I won't. It took too long to pick all the papers up yesterday," Jordyn said.

"Do you want me to help you carry something?" Emma asked.

"No, you have enough books to carry. But thanks for asking," Jordyn said.

"I'll be glad to help," Emma said.

Jordyn said, "That's okay. Just help me pick up my things if I drop them." Then she laughed. And Emma laughed too.

The two girls quickly walked to the car. And they got in the car.

Emma's mom said, "Did you both have a good day?"

"Yes," the girls said at the same time.

Emma said, "I thought we'd have a math test this week. But we won't have it until next week. I'm sure glad about that."

"I'm glad too," Jordyn said.

Emma and Jordyn were in the same math class.

Jordyn said, "And I don't have any other tests this week. That means I'll have more time to get ready for the debate."

Emma's mom said, "I'm glad you don't have any tests this week, Jordyn. But make sure you do all of your homework for your classes. And don't spend too much time on work for the debate."

"I'll do all of my homework. But I have to do a lot for the debate. I want to do as well as I can next week," Jordyn said.

Emma's mom said, "I'm sure you'll do your best."

And Emma was sure Jordyn would too.

But would Trenton High be able to beat Camden High?

chapter 4

It was Friday morning. Emma was in her math class. It was almost time for class to start. But Jordyn wasn't there.

Then Jordyn hurried into the classroom. She quickly walked over to her desk. And she sat down.

Emma looked over at Jordyn. She said, "Why were you almost late, Jordyn?"

"I saw Mrs. Chen in the hall. And she wanted to talk to me," Jordyn said.

"About what?" Emma asked.

"She wants me to stop by her room on

the way to lunch. She wants to talk to me about the debate next week. I wonder why," Jordyn said. She looked worried.

"Don't worry about it, Jordyn," Emma said. But she knew Jordyn would.

The bell rang to start class. And Emma and Jordyn couldn't talk any more.

The girls had a lot of class work to do. So the class time went by quickly for Emma.

The end of class bell rang.

Jordyn quickly got up from her desk. And she looked over at Emma. She said, "I have to talk to Mrs. Chen. I'll meet you at lunch."

"Okay," Emma said.

Jordyn hurried out of the classroom.

Emma got up from her desk. And she walked out of the classroom. Then she went to the lunchroom.

Emma got her lunch. And she went over to a table. She sat down.

A few minutes later, she saw Jordyn come into the lunchroom. And Jordyn looked upset.

Jordyn quickly got her lunch. Then she hurried over to the table. And she sat down.

Emma said, "What's wrong, Jordyn?"

She hoped Mrs. Chen didn't pull Jordyn off of the debate team. But she didn't know of any reason why Mrs. Chen would do that. So she didn't think that was why Jordyn looked upset.

Jordyn said, "I guess I should be happy about this. But I'm not."

"What are you talking about, Jordyn? And why aren't you happy if you should be happy? That doesn't make sense," Emma said.

"I know," Jordyn said.

"So what are you talking about? What did Mrs. Chen say? Hurry up and tell me," Emma said.

"Mrs. Chen wants me and not Seth to debate Darius one on one. I can never beat Darius," Jordyn said.

Emma said, "Mrs. Chen must think you have a chance to beat Darius. Or she wouldn't let a junior debate one on one with him."

"I know I should think that. But I don't. I'm sure Darius will beat me," Jordyn said.

"But that's just it, Jordyn. You don't know that for sure. So don't think that way," Emma said.

"I know you're right. But I can't help but think that," Jordyn said.

"Practice a lot. And just do the best you can. Camden High can't win all of its debates," Emma said.

"I know. But I want Trenton High to win the state finals. And I don't think we can if I debate Darius," Jordyn said.

Emma hoped Jordyn could beat Darius. But she wasn't sure Jordyn could.

Emma said, "There's always next year, Jordyn. And I'm sure you'll be on the team then too. And you'll have another chance to win the state finals."

"You're right. There's always next year. And Darius won't be on the Camden High team then. He'll be in college. But I want to win now. And not have to wait for another chance to win," Jordyn said.

Emma wanted Trenton High to win this year too. And she wished there was a way for her to help Jordyn.

chapter 5

It was Friday night. Almost seven o'clock. Emma was home. She was waiting for Darius. They had a date. They were going to a play at Camden High.

The front doorbell rang. Emma hurried to the door. She quickly opened it.

Darius said, "I hope I'm not too early."

"You aren't. Do you want to come in?" Emma asked.

"No, thanks. I think we should go on to the play. I heard that it's good. And I want to get a good seat. So I think we should get there early," Darius said.

Emma stood on the porch. And she closed the front door.

Then she and Darius started to walk to his car. Emma was glad that it was still light. It was easy to see where she was walking.

Darius said, "Do you have a lot of homework this weekend?"

"No. Not much. How about you?" Emma asked.

"About the same as I always have. Too much," Darius said.

"Do you have a test Monday?" Emma asked.

"No. But the big debate is next week. And I have a lot of work to do for that," Darius said.

"I know how much you like being on the debate team. So I know you don't mind homework like that," Emma said.

"You're right about that," Darius said.

Emma and Darius got in his car.

Emma saw a big folder. It was in the middle of the front seat. It had a lot of papers in it.

Darius started the car. And he started to drive down the road.

Emma looked down at the folder. She said, "What's in this big folder? It looks a lot like the folder Jordyn has. She keeps her debate stuff in it."

Darius said, "It's my debate folder. I forgot to take it in the house when I got home today."

"Jordyn and I were walking to Mom's car. And Jordyn dropped her folder on the ground. I helped her pick up the papers. She really had a lot of stuff in it. I guess your folder is a lot like hers," Emma said.

"Do you want to look at it?" Darius asked.

That surprised Emma. "Yes," she said. She was sure that was what Darius wanted her to say.

Emma picked up the folder. She opened it. And she started to look at the papers. Most of the papers were research Darius had done for the team.

Then Emma saw some pages about the members of the Trenton High team.

Did Darius forget they were in his folder?

"Is it okay for me to look at all of this?" Emma asked.

"Sure," Darius said.

One page was about Jordyn. And Emma started to read it. It was about her strong points when she debated. And it was about her weak points when she debated. And it had some ideas about how to beat Jordyn in a debate.

Then Emma found another page. And she started to read it. It was a page of notes Darius had written about himself. And it listed his strong and weak points when he debated.

Emma read all of the notes. Then she closed the folder. And she put it back on the front seat between her and Darius.

She said, "You've done a lot of work, Darius."

"Yeah, I have," Darius said.

Darius sounded very proud of himself. And Emma thought he should be proud of himself.

Darius said, "I think we'll win the debate next week. But I'm sorry we have to beat your school to win."

Emma didn't think Darius should be so sure his team would win. She had read what he put in the folder about himself.

And what he put about Jordyn.

Maybe she had found a way to help Jordyn. And Trenton High.

Emma could hardly wait until tomorrow morning. She would call Jordyn as soon as she could. She had too much to say to text. And she would tell Jordyn what she had found out. Then maybe Jordyn could beat Darius in the debate.

chapter 6

It was the next morning. Emma got up early. She ate her breakfast quickly.

Emma hurried to her bedroom. And she called Jordyn on her cell phone. She was in a hurry to talk to Jordyn. She wanted to tell Jordyn what she'd read in Darius's debate folder.

Jordyn answered on the first ring. She said, "Hi, Emma. How was your date last night?"

"Great. How was your date?" Emma asked.

Jordyn had a date with a boy in their math class. And it was the first time she had dated him.

Jordyn said, "I had fun. I hope Jacob asks me for another date."

"I'm glad you had fun with Jacob," Emma said. "He's cute."

"I thought you'd call this morning to find out about my date with Jacob. But I didn't think you'd call this early," Jordyn said.

"I wanted to know about your date. But that's not why I called," Emma said.

"Oh? Why did you call?" Jordyn asked. She sounded surprised.

"I found out something last night. And I can't wait to tell you," Emma said.

"What? I can't wait to hear," Jordyn said.

"You won't believe what I got to look

at last night. And I read some of it," Emma said.

"What? Hurry and tell me. So I won't have to wonder what it was," Jordyn said.

"I hope it'll help you. And I think it will," Emma said.

Then Emma's mom came into the bedroom. She said, "I didn't know you were on the phone, Emma. Who're you talking to?"

"Jordyn," Emma said.

"Tell Jordyn you have to hang up. I want you to do something for me. And you can call her back later," Emma's mom said.

"Can I talk to Jordyn for a few more minutes, Mom? I really need to tell her something," Emma said.

"I'm sure it can wait, Emma. I need to buy some things at the store. And I want you to go with me. So you can help me carry them," her mom said.

"I need to talk only a few more minutes, Mom," Emma said.

Her mom said, "I want you to hang up now, Emma. You've all afternoon to talk to Jordyn. And we need to go now. I need to get back here in time to cook lunch. So hang up."

"Okay, Mom," Emma said.

Her mom said, "And turn off your cell phone until we get back. You know I don't want you to talk or text when we go somewhere."

"Okay, Mom," Emma said.

Jordyn said, "What's going on, Emma?"

Emma said, "I have to hang up now, Jordyn. And I have to turn off my cell phone. Mom wants me to go to the store with her. I'll call you as soon as I get home."

"Can't you tell me now, Emma? I can't wait to find out what you looked at. And how it might help me," Jordyn said.

Emma's mom was still in the room. And Emma knew she had to hang up.

"Sorry, Jordyn. I have to hang up. But I'll call you as soon as I get home," Emma said.

Emma wanted to tell Jordyn then. But she knew her mom was in a hurry.

Jordyn would have to wait to find out Emma's news. But Emma was sure Jordyn would be happy when she found out.

chapter 7

It was the same morning. Emma had just gotten home from the store. Her mom bought a lot. And Emma helped her carry all of it into the house.

Emma was still in a hurry to talk to Jordyn. And she was sure Jordyn was in a hurry to talk to her.

Emma said, "Is it okay if I go to my room, Mom? And call Jordyn?"

"Yes, Emma. And thanks for all of the help," her mom said.

"Glad to help," Emma said.

Then Emma hurried into her bedroom. And she quickly turned on her cell phone. But her cell phone rang before she could call Jordyn.

Emma saw it was Darius. She quickly answered it.

Darius said, "Hi, Emma. Do you have time to talk?"

"Sure. And I'm glad you called. I had a great time last night," Emma said.

"Me too," Darius said. But he didn't really sound like he did.

Emma wondered why. She said, "Is everything okay, Darius?"

"Yeah, sure. But I need to talk to you about something," Darius said.

"What?" Emma asked.

Emma thought Darius sounded upset. But she wasn't sure.

"It's about last night," Darius said.

"What about it?" Emma asked.

Emma thought their date was good. She had fun on the date. And she thought Darius did too. So she didn't know any reason why Darius would be upset about it.

But maybe Emma only thought he sounded upset. Maybe he really wasn't upset.

Darius said, "I know I don't have a reason to worry about this." Darius stopped talking. And he didn't seem to want to say any more.

Why didn't he want to say more? That made Emma worry.

Emma said, "What are you worried about, Darius?" She hoped it wasn't about something she'd done.

"I know I don't really have a reason to worry about this. But I have been worrying about it. So that's why I called you," Darius said.

"So what is it, Darius? Please tell me. You are starting to make me worry too," Emma said.

Darius said, "It's about your friend Jordyn. I know she's on the Trenton High debate team."

Emma didn't say anything.

Darius sounded like he'd just found out about Jordyn. But he'd known that for a long time. So Emma knew that wasn't why he'd called her.

But now Emma thought she knew why Darius called. And what he was worried about. He was worried she would tell Jordyn what she'd read in his debate folder.

Darius said, "I know Jordyn is your best friend, Emma. And I know you girls tell each other everything."

"Not everything," Emma said. But she and Jordyn did tell each other almost everything.

Darius said, "You go to Trenton High, Emma. And Camden High debates them next week. So I should never have let you look at my debate folder."

Emma thought Darius was right about that. She would never have told him anything about the Trenton High team. And he should never have let her see his folder.

Darius said, "You won't tell Jordyn what you read in my folder, will you?"

Emma didn't say anything.

Then Darius said, "I'm sorry I asked you that, Emma. I know you wouldn't do that. I don't trust all girls. But I do trust you," Darius said.

But Darius shouldn't trust her. Emma did plan to tell Jordyn. She wanted to do all that she could to help Jordyn.

chapter 8

Emma had just gotten off the phone with Darius. And she started to call Jordyn. But she couldn't do it. At least not yet. She had to think about it before she did.

Darius trusted her. So how could she tell Jordyn what she'd read in his debate folder?

Emma didn't want to call Jordyn right then. And she didn't want Jordyn to call or text her. So she turned off her cell phone. And she went to the kitchen to talk to her mom.

Her mom said, "You didn't talk to Jordyn very long."

"I didn't call her. I want to talk to you before I do," Emma said.

Her mom looked surprised. "Why?" her mom asked.

Emma told her mom about what she'd read in Darius's debate folder.

Then Emma said, "I was going to tell Jordyn what I'd read. But Darius just called me."

Then Emma told her mom that Darius didn't want her to tell Jordyn. And she told her mom what Darius said about trusting her.

Her mom said, "What about now, Emma? Do you still plan to tell Jordyn?"

"I don't know. That's why I want to talk to you. What do you think I should do?" Emma asked.

Her mom said, "What did Darius tell you last night? Did he say you couldn't tell anyone what you saw in his folder?"

"No. He didn't say I had to keep what I saw a secret. But now he wants me to do that. What should I do, Mom? Should I tell Jordyn? Or should I keep it a secret?" Emma asked.

"I can't tell you what to do, Emma. That's up to you. But I know you'll do what's right," her mom said.

"But I don't know what I should do. Darius trusts me. But Jordyn is my best friend. And I want to help her. I care about Darius. But I want Jordyn to win the debate. And I want Trenton High to win," Emma said.

"You have a hard choice to make, Emma. And I can't tell you what to do. Just do what you think is right," her mom said.

But it was hard to know what was right. Darius should never have let her see his debate folder. But he trusted her.

And Jordyn was her best friend. And she wanted to help Jordyn all that she could.

Emma kept thinking about what she should do. And then she knew what she should do. It wasn't about friendship. It was really a matter of trust.

Could she be trusted?

The phone rang.

Her mom said, "I'm busy, Emma. Please answer the phone for me."

Emma didn't want to talk on the phone right then. But she answered the phone.

Jordyn said, "So you are home, Emma. Why didn't you call me? You said you would call me as soon as you got home. I've been trying to call you on your cell phone. But you still have it turned off."

"I'm sorry, Jordyn. I should've called you," Emma said.

"What did you find out last night? And how do you think it will help me? I can hardly wait to know," Jordyn said.

"Darius has been doing a lot of research. And I thought it would help you to know that," Emma said.

"I know Darius has done a lot of research. All of us on the debate teams do a lot of research. Is that all you had to tell me?" Jordyn asked. Jordyn sounded surprised.

"Yes," Emma said.

Emma wanted to tell Jordyn what she had read in Darius's folder. But she couldn't do it. It was a matter of trust. And not of friendship.

consider this...

1. Would you betray one friend to another friend?

2. What would you do if you saw something that you shouldn't have seen?

3. Have you ever been trusted with a secret?

4. Did Darius make a mistake when he let Emma look at his papers?

5. Is trust more important than friendship?